Hairy Maclary's
SHOWBUSINESS

Lynley Dodd

Spindlewood

In Riverside Hall
on Cabbage Tree Row,
the Cat Club were having
their Annual Show.

There were fat cats
and thin cats,
tabbies and greys,
kick-up-a-din cats
with boisterous ways.
Cooped up in cages,
they practised their wails
while their owners fussed over
their teeth
and their
tails.

Out in the street,
tied to a tree,
Hairy Maclary
was trying to see.
He struggled and squirmed,
he unravelled the knot
and dragging his lead,
he was off
at the
trot.

He bounced up the steps,
he pounced through the door,
he pricked up his ears
and he pranced round the floor;
flapping and flustering,
bothering,
blustering,
leaving behind him
a hiss
and a
roar.

'STOP!'
cried the President,
'COLLAR HIM, QUICK!'
But Hairy Maclary
was slippery slick.

He slid under tables,

he jumped over chairs,

he skittered through legs

and he sped down the stairs.

In and out doorways,
through banners and flags,

tangling together
belongings and bags.

Along came Miss Plum
with a big silver cup.
'GOT HIM!' she said
as she snaffled him up.

LONGEST
WHISKERS

SNOOTIEST

BIGGEST
FAMILY

WORST
TEMPER

Preening and purring,
the prizewinners sat
with their rosettes and cups
on the prizewinners' mat...

and WHO
won the prize
for the SCRUFFIEST CAT?

Hairy Maclary
from Donaldson's Dairy.

British Library
Cataloguing in Publication Data

Dodd, Lynley
  Hairy Maclary's Showbusiness
  1. Title
  823 [J]

Published in 1991 by Spindlewood.

First published in Mini-Spin edition
in 1994 by Spindlewood
70, Lynhurst Avenue, Barnstaple, Devon EX31 2HY

Both editions first published by
Mallinson Rendel Publishers Ltd,
P.O. Box 9409, Wellington.

© Lynley Dodd 1991

ISBN 0-907349-92-7

Typeset in New Zealand.
Printed and bound by Colorcraft Ltd, Hong Kong.